Sailing off to Sleep

by Linda Ashman   illustrated by Susan Winter

Simon & Schuster Books for Young Readers
New York   London   Toronto   Sydney   Singapore

Special thanks to Adelina ("Dee Dee"), who keeps things sailing smoothly

–L. A.

SIMON & SCHUSTER BOOKS FOR YOUNG READERS
An imprint of Simon & Schuster Children's Publishing Division
1230 Avenue of the Americas, New York, New York 10020

Book design by Jennifer Reyes
The text of this book is set in Clearface.
The illustrations are rendered in watercolor and Aquarelle pencil.
Printed in Hong Kong
2 4 6 8 10 9 7 5 3 1
Library of Congress Cataloging-in-Publication Data
Ashman, Linda.
Sailing off to sleep / by Linda Ashman ; illustrated by Susan Winter.
p. cm.
Summary: Bedtime for a little one brings an imaginary journey
to the North Pole to cuddle and play with the many animals there.
ISBN 0-689-82971-X
[1. Zoology—Arctic regions—Fiction. 2. North Pole—Fiction.
3. Imagination—Fiction. 4. Bedtime—Fiction. 5. Stories in rhyme.]
I. Winter, Susan, ill. II.Title.
PZ8.3.H5344 Sai 2001
[E]--dc21
99-047055

To Jackson, who had me thinking of polar bears in the middle of some cold winter nights
—L. A.

To Felicia
—S. W.

It's nighttime, my little one.
Climb into bed.

I don't want to sleep—
I'll go sailing instead.

There's only one problem:
Your ship has no sail.

I'm tying my boat
to the tail of a whale.

Where will you go
with this blubbery beast?

As far as we can—
to the Arctic, at least!

The ocean is icy—
you might sink your boat!

I'll ask a fat walrus
to keep me afloat.

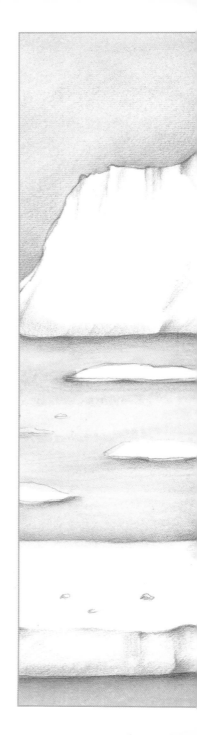

Won't you be cold?
It's freezing up there!

I'll cuddle up close
to a warm polar bear.

What about food?
You'll get hungry, my sweet.

I can make ice cream!
There's plenty to eat.

The wind can be fierce—
you'll be tossed like a ball.

I'll land on a fur seal—
it won't hurt at all.

What if you're lost?
You don't know the way.

I'll follow the tracks
of a caribou sleigh.

You won't have your playmates
to chase in this place.

I'll take on some auks
in an ice-skating race.

What if you trip?

It's slippery, you know.

I'll ride on a moose.
They're used to the snow.

Won't you get lonely
out there on your own?

The wolf pups are friendly.
I won't be alone.

But what if I miss you?
(I already do!)

I'll find a big snow goose
and fly home to you.

*And what will you do
when you're back in my sight?*

I'll climb in your arms
and I'll kiss you good night.

I guess you should go—
there's a long night ahead.

Maybe tomorrow . . .

I'm ready for bed.